I0547196

Seek Me In The Orange

Cover Design: Madison Archer
Illustration: Madison Archer

First Edition: 2024

Paperback ISBN: 979-8-9907939-0-3
Hardback ISBN: 979-8-9907939-2-7
E Book ISBN: 979-8-9907939-1-0

Published by Madison Archer
6001 W. Parmer Ln Suite 370
P.O. Box #73
Austin, Texas 78727
madisonarcher.com

Seek Me In The Orange

Madison Archer

Seek Me In The Orange

By Madison Archer

Madison Archer

Seek Me In The Orange

For my Nana,
I love you.

Introduction

Seek Me In The Orange was born at the end of one of the worst periods of my life. I spent year after year locked into a state of constant change and uncertainty, barely able to rest long enough to process my experiences. This book is the breath of relief I felt once my world finally stopped spinning. It is the looking around me to see that everything had changed fundamentally, permanently, in unprecedented ways. It is the shocked laughter bubbling out of my chest when I realized I had survived something that I thought would take me out. It is life-sustaining gratitude that has filled me in the moments since.

I write this book for everyone caught in their own whirlwind to let you know that it won't last forever. Life can be unpredictable but one thing you can always count on is the cycles of nature that repeat season after season. Some are long, cold winter nights and others are gentle, blushing spring mornings. Sometimes we are caught in the buzzing blaze of summer afternoons and then we settle into cool, cozy autumn twilights.

Seek Me In The Orange is an ode to these changes and the bright, shimmering orange joy I've found within them. May it help lead you to yours.

Content Warning: Mentions of death and grief in Chapter 2.

Seek Me In The Orange

Madison Archer

Table of Contents

I. - Lessons in Magical Thinking

II. - When the Magic Died

III. - The Crossroads

Madison Archer

I.

Lessons In Magical Thinking

Dear Reader

Do your eyes search for silver linings,
Or are they enamored with the dark?

Do you yearn for new beginnings,
Just to get frightened by the spark?

There's no need to cry about endings,
When there's always a new start.

I could be there to hold your hand,
If you let me into your heart.

My Grandmother Is A Witch

Do you remember the time when
I ate too much raw cookie dough on Christmas Eve
Stomach churning, you said you told me so.
I slept on the couch that night
So I could hold your cold hand and you said
"Do you know what the last three letters
In 'cold' are? Old." You liked to remind me.

2 hour drives through the woods to your house
Always seemed to take forever until
The crunch of the gravel driveway,
Red Pontiac, blue house, pink carpet in the bathroom.
You washed my hair with rose shampoo,
Tucked me into the trundle bed next to yours
And read me stories about witches who
Could fly anywhere they wanted to.

You said we had to run real fast, big splashes
Though the rain because it makes witches melt
And you were born on Halloween. So we
Collected orange flowers and put them
On our witches fingers, casting spells on
On the clouds so they would never
Cry big, thunderstorm tears again.

Under sunshine we planted tulip bulbs,
Pastel yellow, pink, purple, blue

In a ring around the Big Tree with the bird feeder
Where the dog keeps digging holes
Looking for treasure hidden on
The other side of the earth if you
Can dig deep enough.
Where you liked to the hide the Easter eggs
On Sunday morning, my church
Shoes stained with discovery.

You took me down to the Mac Donald's
Golden Arches, golden fries in sets of two
Dipped in ketchup on the table by the playground.
Rocking back n' forth on the swings until
I was flying so high I saw an angel
Among the clouds who looked like you,
All there except for a black cat, a magic broom.

I learned to tell time by hallmark cards
Written in your hand on every holiday
Red envelopes in the mailbox, glitter stickers
A twenty tucked inside, traded in for
A new paperback with the fresh book smell
That reminded me of your house,
A little magic to get me by until
Next summer.

Texas Tea

From the pot
To the pitcher
To the glass,
Sweeter than
Grandma's
Birthday cash.

Dear Jennifer

I didn't mean to pull your hair like that,
It's more that I was enchanted by its shine
Within these shadowed halls where
Children wear uniforms and walk in straight lines.

I didn't like when you copied my colors,
You painted your Jesus orange just like mine.
When every girl in Miss Fuller's room copied you,
My fingers curled a fist around my hemline.

I sat down next to you in music class
Because it was the seat I was assigned,
You liked to tell everyone how I followed you
To the beat of a practiced punchline.

When we said our prayers at lunch that day
Your voice drowned mine out by design.
I stared at your hair in earnest now,
Golden, beautiful, straight from your hairline.

The difference between villain and victim
Has always been a hazy, blurry line,
No one believed it was an accident
When I pulled your hair the second time.

The Book That Saved Me

It began with eight dollars at the bookstore.
A blue-green cover, a bright red cat, a promise
Of a new home to be found in wild places.

I slipped between the pages until I dropped them
In the bathtub, on rain soaked concrete,
But by then it was too late. I would never let go.

I read at the lunch table, in the car, when my
Parents moved me from home to home and
Every other place that I would rather not be.

I didn't notice the screaming in the other room,
The shattered glass in the hallways, the way
They begged me to pay attention in class.

I escaped into the night, waded through swollen rivers,
Battled against hidden enemies and searched
For caves filled with stars and moonlight.

I saved the day, I earned a brand new name
And so it didn't matter what they called me
In the time between each paragraph and page.

One blue-green book, a bright red cat, a promise
Of an escape, a life that only be saved when
One dares to believe in worlds unseen.

4th House

When Jupiter left, he took the sun with him.
Mercury fell from the sky, the silver of his eyes
Burning into mine and I was lost.
I don't know this land, these trees, they weren't
Made for me and my fumbling hands in the dark.
I think I must have been stolen from
My true home, where the water always satisfies
And spirit speaks in dew drops on spider webs.
I search for meaning in broken branches,
Polluted rivers, the dead bird on the sidewalk
And the only thing to learn is death comes
Like an old friend, over and over again.

The Yellow Cloud of Doom

Beware! Beware!
The yellow cloud of doom!
The way it imitates the sunlight,
The way it blocks out the moon.
The sticky pollen powder
Springing forth when flowers bloom,
Drifting through the atmosphere
Like a deadly vapor fume.

Beware! Beware!
The yellow cloud of doom!
It will snatch away your happiness,
Leave you hiding in your room.
It's rolling through the country side
Looking for people to consume.
Just a little bit will take you down,
Just less than a teaspoon.

Beware! Beware!
The yellow cloud of doom!
When you hear the songbirds calling,
You know it will be upon you soon.
Unfurling like a noxious gas
Exploding in lemon plume,
Beware! Beware!
The yellow cloud of doom!

Leaf Me Alone

The huckleberry towers into the clouds
Branches bowing low among the grass,
Bark as thick as my mother's skin,
Roots burrowed deep enough to last.
The leaves love to whisper to me
And the songbirds like to sing,
If all I've seen is all I've come to know
Then I don't know a god damn thing.

II.

When The Magic Died

Boots

The whole world has moved on
But I'm stuck in this grave with you
They must have buried me too
Because I can't quite seem to shake
The loneliness left in your wake
I watch the clouds drift by
And assign them all your name
Daring them to conjure up
A visage of your face
It should have been carved into a mountain
The kind nobody can replace
Sketched into the stars somehow
A constellation I can trace

You left me with the embers
You left me with your ashes
You left me without the will
To get out of bed and put on my glasses
Without you the world is just a blur
Nothing here makes sense
All distorted shapes and circumstance
The colors too intense
You took my glasses with you
Right into your grave
I don't think I can see anything now
Except the way I was made

Seek Me In The Orange

All sports cars and motorcycles
Women with tongues like knives
I'm made of dry Texas soil
Fried chicken and French fries
I think I could be different now
Since the world has forced me to be
Without you I'm a different person
And I don't know how to be me
I use to think it was a good thing
To spread all over the world
Use to think I wanted to be
A kaleidoscope color swirl
But ever since the day you left me
All I've wanted is my roots
To feel some familiar ground
Tread underneath my boots.

It's Just Me and Mac N Cheese

Against the world.
Thick, creamy cheddar,
Nimble noodles sliding
Together.
The bowl, the living room,
Golden yellow on
A dark day.

The Sound Of Your Voice

Could stitch up the rift of any earthquake.
It's seismic, crackled with age but heart holding,
Wrapped in warm vanilla sugar,
Stretching across miles of lands we call home,
But will never feel quite right
Without the sing song notes of childhood stories
Sung along to your favorite tune,
Elvis, Brad Paisley, and
All the birds of June.

The Visitation

Last night

> I asked a ghost
> If he remembered me,
> Like death could
> Steal memories
> The way it does
> The body.

I wonder about

> The permanence
> Of a soul,
> Of a connection,
> About the way
> A dream can feel
> More real
> than I do.

He told me

> I should have
> Taken more
> Pictures,
> That my old dog
> Lives with
> Someone else.
> They're happy.

The Shadow

Oh, how the sun will rise and dig the dreams from my eyes,

Harvesting memories and subconscious white lies,

Swirling into the dregs of my coffee,

Swallowed by brain fog, tough like toffee

Stuck between my teeth, it's impossible to leave

These parts of myself behind,

No matter how hard I try.

Compartmentalize

Physically I am:
Sitting at the red light, engine rumbling
Windows down and volume on high,
Becoming one with the shake and quake
Of the Austin highway, married to the moment.

Mentally I am:
Somewhere on a back road in Beaumont
On my knees in front of the gravestones
Absent of the ruby red roses for your mother
You aren't around to drop off anymore.
Throat aching, parched and sore,
Gaping, unknowable void in my chest.
You know that I can't rest the same,
You know that no matter where I am,
Every sound echoes your name.

Evidence Of My Grief

Marches through the trenches of Texas,
Lingers in the meadows of Pennsylvania
And down the vertebrae of my spine.

It swallows the silence whole like a sugar powdered donut,
Sitting heavy in the depths of my stomach
Like generations of heart disease.

It stacks piles and piles of cardboard boxes in my closet,
Full of pictures and letters and little stuffed owls,
Hiding skeletons and a suitcase of heartbreak.

It decorates the ornaments on my Christmas tree
Like a tiny football player and a Coca Cola polar bear,
Illuminated and yet so often, overlooked.

Messages (11:11)

When Sharin passed she left autumn butterflies
Saffron wings glittering in the morning breeze,
Like the permanent ink that claimed her shoulder.

When Ruby passed she left the doting spiders
Spinning delicate webs with loopy patterns,
Like the crochet laid upon her rocking chair.

When Daniel passed he left the motorcycles
Racing down the highway under sunbeams,
Like his blue Harley headed to ocean shores.

When Micheal passed he left the Dallas stars
Sterling silver, navy blue across night skies,
Like guiding lights I can always follow home.

When I pass I will leave behind all my words
Across notebooks, digital journals of code,
Tender love letters only you can perceive.

Release

Flames like feathers, scattered
Eating up the ethers
Saffron wings
Encompass and collapse
Dilapidated structures
Piles of monochrome ash
Spread across the gulf
Pushing, pulling, tugging
Drifting on a tidal wave
Under ivory nimbus
And glowing sun beams,
Passing through the lips
Of dolphins.

I watch the ocean glimmer
With your essence
Forevermore.

Madison Archer

III.

The Crossroads

Lost

There's one egg missing from
        the dozen,
Everyone is here except that
        one cousin.

There's a empty space here that
        needs filling,
There's a loneliness here that
        needs killing.

Dull fog replaces memories in
        your head,
Can't remember who's missing from
        your bed.

You can't find something you forgot
        you lost,
But it doesn't stop you from feeling
        the cost.

The Crossroads

My soul met yours at the crossroads
Between what could be and should have been.
Two cars meant to collide pass each other by
Under the low hum of the street light.

My eyes caught yours through the window
Showing me all that we leave behind.
As your colors fade to black against the sky,
I watch red bulbs escape into the night.

I hold vigil for you on the sidewalk
Knowing lightning won't strike me twice.
There's a yearning in me I can't deny,
A love that never got to take flight.

I recreate your face in the shadows,
Crystal visions, never quite right.
Two souls at the crossroads, meant to collide
Don't - I wish I could tell you why.

I Fixed Her

When I speak, no one listens -
Like the silence of the kitchen at 3am
Waiting for life to begin again with the sunrise.
I can't bring myself to meet their eyes,
To see what they make of me.
The illusion they form in their minds,
The inevitable conclusion is never kind.
I am more than their perceptions,
The face you see is mere deception.
This body could never hold the whole truth.
It's too small, too mundane to
Deserve a second a glance, a first chance
To change permanent minds.
My truth is stuck in my throat and
My throat is glued to hands that don't notice
The pulse under their fingers
Until it eventually stops.

Sand Castles

I don't forgive and forget, I ruminate-
Over think, pull apart and recalculate.
How many jokes until I make you laugh?
How many laughs until you like me?
How many times can I say the honest truth
Before this thing falls apart in my hands?
If friendships were castles mine would
All be made out of Galveston sand.
I spend hours carving windows and walkways,
Line them with seashells and bits of glass
Just to watch the ocean destroy it all.
It's never an "if," but always a "when."
When you get tired of me trying too hard,
When my back story gets a little too graphic,
When I hold your hand a little too tight,
When you get a funny feeling and decide
To just let it all fade, instead of asking why.
Why is for me to ask, when I stare at this horizon
As I picture what could be among the waves.
Why is it so hard to build connection?
Why haven't I learned any new jokes?
Why does it always inevitably end this way?

Misinterpretation

Loving you was like

Singing my favorite song;

10 years on the radio, my stereo

Too loud to know I was singing the lyrics

Wrong.

You Don't Inspire Me Anymore

I use to dream of the oak tree that would spring
From the tiny little acorn seed.
I use to imagine the wind that would rustle
The rainbow of a hundred thousand leaves.
When I looked at you I saw sketch upon sketch,
Immortalizing the way a body can stretch.
I saw all of the ways a heart can catch a feeling,
Spin out of control, reeling into artistic impression.
But all I saw was all that you denied, I tried
To keep drawing but the ink in my pen had dried.
There is no love to spring from this depression,
Never an answer to any of my questions.
To be inspired requires the acceptance of desire,
To move beyond the barest of your needs to see
What could have become of our tiny acorn seed.
All that you denied yourself, you also took from me.

Mend

I keep trying to write you poems,
But there is hardly anything to put to paper
        anymore.
I use to wait and wait by the window, I use to hold open
        the door.
You never came nor sent a letter,
There hasn't even been a whisper in
        the wind.
At some point I've come to accept that some things
        are never meant to mend.

Starfish

I wish I was a starfish
So I could grow a new hand.
I'd finally buy that drum kit
Maybe even start a band.

Perhaps I'd become a sports star,
I've always liked volley ball.
I think I'd take up archery
And shoot from castle walls.

I'd learn to ride on horse back,
Race toward a new horizon.
I'd paint canvas after canvas
Until my body begins to wizen.

I'd finally use all that yarn
The crochet needles in the bin,
Forgotten craft project corpses
Would learn to live again.

I wouldn't put off the dishes
The to-do list would be done.
Never again would I feel guilty
For just soaking up the sun.

Madison Archer

If I could grow a new hand
There is nothing I wouldn't do.
If only a body could be mended
With papier mache and glue.

I wish I was a starfish
I'd play all day in the sand,
Blowing bubbles in the water
Never worried about a hand.

IV.

Rekindling

Things Cats Won't Tell You

More often than not, curiosity is
Psychologically damaging
And nine lives isn't long enough
To learn how to stop flinching
At every unexpected noise.
You could search forever and
Never find the place you are from,
Walk the entire city and
Find a hundred cozy homes
Bursting with free food and still
Crave the thrill of sinking
Your claws into the soft flesh
Of the mouse in the alleyway.
The water is cold but it always dries,
The night is dark but you were made for it
And it's the sun that puts us to sleep.
Trees are never all that tall
Until you try to climb down
And the worst that could ever happen
Is landing right side down.

When I Say I'm Bisexual,

What I really mean is that I don't care about sex at all / I have
no concern for the secrets under your clothes / from the color
of your hair / to the polish on your toes.

What I really mean is that I tend to fall in love with everyone /
and I'm always willing to see where it goes / I always have room
for more love, more compassion, more intimacy / and there's
no pressure to already know.

What I really mean is that I loved you before the day we met /
and I'll love every incarnation we've yet to meet / My love for
you can't be contained in any words / on any page / I will love
you in every moment / in every body / and through every age.

Wings

Can my wings still fly
Weighed down by a lifetime
Of never quite right or not enough,
Of way too much all at once?

Can my wings still fly
Shredded by the sunlight,
A sharp tongue, a gutting knife,
Featherless and fright?

Can my wings still fly
Molded by the magazine,
As if they've always been
A bullet hole mosaic?

New Moon

Love is when I plant seeds right where I am,
In soil that has never produced anything before
And water it with the hopes and dreams
I've been told to put to rest by now,
But haven't.
I believe everything can be recycled if
I wait for the right moment to come.

Some would call it hoarding to cling to
The little bits and pieces I can't quite fit
Into the picture perfect life I've been sold,
But I call it patience.
I plant my patience too and learn to be bored.
To find love in leaves falling on a cold day,
To feel it in the crunch under my boots,
In the caterpillar racing across the sidewalk
And acorns cracked open on the ground.

I plant my uncertainty and hope it blooms
Into something that looks like confidence.
I plant my anxiety and pray it grows into
The comfort I once found in my mothers arms.
I sit by my garden and sing to it every morning
While I feed it all of my what ifs and maybes,
All of my would have, could have, should haves.
I let the soil soak up tears born of heartbreaks
I've spent too much time contemplating
And ask the earth to turn it into love.

Seek Me In The Orange

Somewhere between winter and spring
I realize that all things grow in their own time
And no amount of begging or pleading can
Alter the course of gestation and force a birth.
I think about the way I was born 2 days early
Because my mother's doctor had a fishing trip
That he could not bear to miss and wonder
Who I might be if I was given the space to decide
When I was ready, to be seen, to be heard, to be loved.

I learn how to measure time in constellations
As they crawl across dark velvet skies.
I study my reflection in the ripples of a river
As the water rushes on toward an ocean I can't see.
I sit on the bank and let it wash dirt from my feet
And marvel at the frogs and the tadpoles
That don't have anywhere else to be.

I find love in the present moment, in the waiting,
In the bits and pieces I hold onto
Just in case they still have something left to give.
I find love in the second chances, in the recycling,
In the death of one thing and the waiting for another.
I find love in the process, in the silence,
In the screaming of the tiny bird who's built
A nest full of babies in my windowsill
As she feeds it the seeds I once planted.

Wardrobe / Resuscitation

These old jeans from high school don't fit
          The way they used to do,
Back when I wrote poetry at bus stops
          In black converse shoes.
Not even my hair color looks right
          Next to this new face.
The girl I used to be has gone
          Missing without a trace.

I can't squeeze inside this dress
          From her 21st birthday,
The old uniform from The Restaurant
          Has long been thrown away.
I can't seem to find that faded sweater
          That use to feel like armor.
I'm left naked in front of the mirror
          Taller, my eyes sharper.

These sweats I've been wearing lately
          Are bursting at the seams.
I've never been this person before,
          I don't know what it means.
I want to grow into a butterfly
          But I'm stuck on caterpillar.
I don't remember who I was before
          I think I must have killed her.

Seek Me In The Orange

I search for her resuscitation
        In a green sun dress,
A clever use of pigmented shadow
        Wipes away the stress.
Perhaps if I wore sandals to the beach
        I could find her there,
Dancing among the sapphire waves
        Wind caressing her hair.

Diviner

It's a novelty to know what I know, to see what I see,
To hear the words from my mind on my lips for free.
I could tell you all about you, things not even
Your mother, your brother, your favorite lover know,
I can make your life into art with one paint brush throw.
There is always a puzzle piece too close to your eye
I reach out and pull it back, the power to demystify
Makes me into quite the enigma, or so they say.
It's not a mystery to me when I do it every day.

The Midnight Ritual

In quiet moments between dawn and midnight
Where clocks never move but change with each glance,
Blank pages transform into dreams unimagined.
The words stuck in my throat become the shadows,
Welcoming me home in the peripheral.
I light the candle and let love possess me,
Moving my tired, broken hand across the page
Without thought, turning sharp weapons into
Silly, squiggly lines under the slow light of sunrise.

Gratitude

Greatness comes in all shapes and sizes
Reminding yourself of this is vital
Awareness of your strengths is more important
Than over analyzing all of your flaws
Invest in your own perspective
Treat your future self like a priority
Use the resources you have right now
Decide that your dreams have always been worth it
Even then, even now, even tomorrow

You'll be glad you did.

V.

On Fire

First Impressions

The first thing I noticed about him
Were the scars criss crossing his fingers,
Up his forearms and reflecting through
The umber of his fire lit eyes.
Something about the distorted tissue
Reminded me of myself somehow,
So I wandered closer without disguise
To watch his movements through the smoke:
         Swift, articulate, dynamic.
He's cool under pressure,
Like a diamond he can't be broken,
Not afraid to be polished by
The landslides of life and all of those
Mistakes, set backs, oh fuck, what nows?
         Precise, efficient, and effective,
Every promise made is a promise kept.
He's a decision maker, disaster correcter,
A quad white mocha latte and a cigarette
Walking circles around his boss
With his head down, humble and sly,
A quiet confidence that can't be denied.
I need to know where it is he goes
When his tires repose upon the concrete,
Who's lap he rests his head on
When the dust settles and why
         Isn't it me?

Orange

I love orange and I love oranges,
Clementine, tangerine, mango
Juice dripping down my face.
Like smooth clover honey
Slathered on buttered bread.

Orange like spring tulips,
Marigolds, pansies, tiger lilies
Glowing in the late afternoon.
Like chrysanthemum petals
Floating onto the sidewalk.

Orange like summer goldfish,
Clown fish, starfish, What the F-fish,
Blowing iridescent bubbles.
Like twirling sea anemone
Dancing in the currents.

Orange like autumn leaves
Pumpkins and Jack-o-lanterns
Heralding the change of seasons.
Like aluminum wrapped candies
Collected in a pillow case.

Seek Me In The Orange

Orange like late winter fires
Flames flickering, shimmering,
A cat with sun stone stripes.
Like lanterns in the darkness
Guiding me back to safety.

Orange like the light of my life,
Sunrise, Sunset, Solar Eclipse,
A holy ring of everlasting fire.
Like the warmth in my chest
Whenever you're around.

The Renaissance Fair

The first time the leaves turned to gold,
We gathered with the dragons and the fae
Between towering oaks and the old highway.
Draped in silks and tanned leather,
With wooden jugs of honey mead in hand,
I drifted over to the palm reader's table,
Clothed in velvet and soft promises,
Little pillows resting on the sand.

With a knowing curve of her lips
She traced the lines on my fingers,
Whispered words that would linger
At the back of my anxious mind:
You will be married for forty long years
And even after that, you will be happy.
To you, the spirits have been kind.

I looked over at you in your kilt,
Tearing through a roasted turkey leg
Waiting for me, sun-drenched shoulders.
In my head I started doing the math,
The kind of calculations that could result
In our feet treading down the same path.

Seek Me In The Orange

Twenty plus forty is sixty years old.
If our relationship lasted that long,
I could be sixty the last time I saw you.
We could grow into wrinkles together
If somehow, we didn't get it wrong.

I realized then that I was greedy,
Because I already knew I wanted more.
More than one year, more than forty,
More than our bodies would allow.

I realized then that I was needy,
Because I needed all of you and then some
And god help me - I needed it now.

A Man Of Solutions

When the engine of her car won't start,
The oil needs changing and
The tires have gone flat,
He pulls out his tool box and
He says "I can fix that."

When the sun has sunk beyond the horizon,
The cold is creeping in and
Broken the thermostat,
He wraps her in his coat and
He says "I can fix that."

When her stomach growls and thunders
Searching for some relief
Between bones and missing fat,
He pulls out his frying pan and
He says "I can fix that."

When the holes in her sweater
Have stretched, threads unraveling
In a blue lit laundromat,
He looks inside his pocket and
He says "I can fix that."

When she jumps further than she can reach,
Ankle wrapped in cactus stings
Blood splashes on the mat,
He tells her to be still and
He says "I can fix that."

When the earth quakes and shudders,
Cracking wide under her feet
And she lands upon her back,
He lifts her into his arms and
He says "I can fix that."

When the stars in her sky begin to fall,
Hopeless and broken
Without a single dream intact,
He pulls out the glue and
He says "I can fix that."

When her heart has been pried open,
Pinned butterfly wings
Shredded beyond future act,
He pulls out his sewing kit and
He says "I can fix even that."

Follow The Clover

There is place out there for the wild hearts,
To rest their exhausted, weary bones.
A place where there is nothing to achieve,
A place from which no one ever roams.
When you become lost with no where to go,
Seek my love, follow the clover home.

Once you enter the hallowed wooden gates,
Never will you find yourself alone.
You can find me waiting in the garden,
By a gentle house of cobbled stone
In the meadow with the wavy wildflowers,
Listening to frogs and crickets groan.

There is no burning asphalt, traffic lights
Or the chirping beeps of a cell phone.
There are no fancy things or shiny toys,
Glimmering like glossy rainbow chrome.
Just the gentle lapping of azure waves,
Orange starfish dancing in the foam.

There is no book of expectations here,
No king posturing or gilded throne.
There is nothing you must do to earn it,
And no guilt for which you must atone.
Just the patterns of our gathered footsteps,
Our kindred bodies have always known.

Seek Me In The Orange

There is a place out there for the wild hearts,
But for many it remains unknown.
For there are no directions to get there,
You find it when your cover is blown.
You've got to let of all that once was,
All of those grand plans must be postponed.

You can find it by following your heart,
Down forest paths the moonlight has shown.
You'll see it once you can no longer stand
The busy life you had once condoned,
When you become lost with no where to go,
Seek my love, follow the clover home.

The Freckle King

I want to pen a hundred romance novels
And write you into the hero every time,
I want to sketch you over and over
And stitch your name into all of my rhymes.

I want to kiss each and every freckle
And worship your body like it's a shrine,
I want to visit your family on the
Holidays and treat it like it's mine.

I want to study the way our hands fit
Together like an intricate design,
I want to keep telling people the story
About how our stars perfectly align.

I want to spend all of my days lamenting
How being loved by you is divine,
I want you to know that whenever you ask,
The answer is always "anytime."

What If I Told You,

That all I do is write love poems
Whenever you're not around?
That I could stream whatever I wanted
But all I need is your gentle sounds.

I like listening to you breathing,
I even like it when you snore.
I like knowing you're in the other room
On the other side of the door.

I want to hear your laughter
Whenever I make a silly joke,
I want to be wherever you are
And hear the words you spoke.

I need more than anything
To hear the thump of your heart beat.
The truth is that without it,
My day feels obsolete.

Til The End

Traverse this hallowed landscape by my side
Imagine the treasures that we could grow
Leafy gardens to feed our children sown

Tenacity and truth I will provide
House of tender love, fireplace aglow
Embrace my wild heart, I'll make it your throne

Eclipses may pass but we won't divide
No mountain too high or valley too low
Devotion from me arrives set in stone

The End

Acknowledgments

I would like give the biggest Thank You Ever to my partner, Sean, who has provided me with the space, time and resources necessary to put together a work such as this. You believed in me long before I ever knew what I wanted to do or how I was going to do it, and never got impatient while I tried to figure it out. You've listened to me talk about this project night after night and encouraged me to keep going. Thank you for being the light of my life.

I would also like to thank my friend and beta reader, Shelby, who has been reading my poetry since we were in middle school. I'm not sure I could have finished this project without your eyes, ears, and helpful comments. At the end of the day, there is anybody out there who gets me or what I'm trying to say quite like you.

Thank you to my Mother and my Nana, who read to me as a child and enabled my obsession with fantasy, the paranormal, and all things magical. My imagination is the best survival tool you've ever given me.

Madison Archer

Madison Archer is a poet and storyteller from Texas, who spent her nomadic childhood scribbling in a notebook on long car rides or lost between the pages of a fantasy novel. Now settled in Austin with her partner, golden retriever and two tabby cats, she spends most of her time writing poems, fantastical worlds, and heart stopping romance. When not typing away for her latest project, you can find her wandering about in nature, dabbling in art, or curled up with her latest read.

Website: madisonarcher.com
Instagram: @madisoninclover
Tik Tok: @madisoninclover

www.ingramcontent.com/pod-product-compliance
Lightning Source LLC
Chambersburg PA
CBHW021936170626
46807CB00007B/3143